The Boxcar Children Mysteries

The Boxcar Children
Surprise Island
The Yellow House Mystery
Mystery Ranch
Mike's Mystery
Blue Bay Mystery
The Woodshed Mystery
The Lighthouse Mystery
Mountain Top Mystery
Schoolhouse Mystery
Caboose Mystery
Houseboat Mystery
Snowbound Mystery
Tree House Mystery
Bicycle Mystery
Mystery in the Sand
Mystery Behind the Wall
Bus Station Mystery
Benny Uncovers a Mystery
The Haunted Cabin Mystery
The Deserted Library Mystery
The Animal Shelter Mystery
The Old Motel Mystery
The Mystery of the Hidden Painting
The Amusement Park Mystery
The Mystery of the Mixed-Up Zoo
The Camp-Out Mystery
The Mystery Girl
The Mystery Cruise
The Disappearing Friend Mystery
The Mystery of the Singing Ghost
The Mystery in the Snow
The Pizza Mystery
The Mystery Horse
The Mystery at the Dog Show
The Castle Mystery
The Mystery of the Lost Village
The Mystery on the Ice
The Mystery of the Purple Pool
The Ghost Ship Mystery
The Mystery in Washington, DC
The Canoe Trip Mystery
The Mystery of the Hidden Beach
The Mystery of the Missing Cat
The Mystery at Snowflake Inn
The Mystery on Stage
The Dinosaur Mystery
The Mystery of the Stolen Music
The Mystery at the Ball Park
The Chocolate Sundae Mystery
The Mystery of the Hot Air Balloon
The Mystery Bookstore
The Pilgrim Village Mystery
The Mystery of the Stolen Boxcar
The Mystery in the Cave
The Mystery on the Train
The Mystery at the Fair
The Mystery of the Lost Mine
The Guide Dog Mystery
The Hurricane Mystery
The Pet Shop Mystery
The Mystery of the Secret Message
The Firehouse Mystery
The Mystery in San Francisco
The Niagara Falls Mystery
The Mystery at the Alamo
The Outer Space Mystery
The Soccer Mystery
The Mystery in the Old Attic
The Growling Bear Mystery
The Mystery of the Lake Monster
The Mystery at Peacock Hall
The Windy City Mystery
The Black Pearl Mystery
The Cereal Box Mystery
The Panther Mystery
The Mystery of the Queen's Jewels
The Stolen Sword Mystery
The Basketball Mystery
The Movie Star Mystery
The Mystery of the Pirate's Map
The Ghost Town Mystery

The Boxcar Children Mysteries

The Mystery of the Black Raven
The Mystery in the Mall
The Mystery in New York
The Gymnastics Mystery
The Poison Frog Mystery
The Mystery of the Empty Safe
The Home Run Mystery
The Great Bicycle Race Mystery
The Mystery of the Wild Ponies
The Mystery in the Computer Game
The Mystery at the Crooked House
The Hockey Mystery
The Mystery of the Midnight Dog
The Mystery of the Screech Owl
The Summer Camp Mystery
The Copycat Mystery
The Haunted Clock Tower Mystery
The Mystery of the Tiger's Eye
The Disappearing Staircase Mystery
The Mystery on Blizzard Mountain
The Mystery of the Spider's Clue
The Candy Factory Mystery
The Mystery of the Mummy's Curse
The Mystery of the Star Ruby
The Stuffed Bear Mystery
The Mystery of Alligator Swamp
The Mystery at Skeleton Point
The Tattletale Mystery
The Comic Book Mystery
The Great Shark Mystery
The Ice Cream Mystery
The Midnight Mystery
The Mystery in the Fortune Cookie
The Black Widow Spider Mystery
The Radio Mystery
The Mystery of the Runaway Ghost
The Finders Keepers Mystery
The Mystery of the Haunted Boxcar
The Clue in the Corn Maze
The Ghost of the Chattering Bones
The Sword of the Silver Knight
The Game Store Mystery
The Mystery of the Orphan Train
The Vanishing Passenger
The Giant Yo-Yo Mystery
The Creature in Ogopogo Lake
The Rock 'n' Roll Mystery
The Secret of the Mask
The Seattle Puzzle
The Ghost in the First Row
The Box That Watch Found
A Horse Named Dragon
The Great Detective Race
The Ghost at the Drive-In Movie
The Mystery of the Traveling Tomatoes
The Spy Game
The Dog-Gone Mystery
The Vampire Mystery
Superstar Watch
The Spy in the Bleachers
The Amazing Mystery Show
The Clue in the Recycling Bin
Monkey Trouble
The Zombie Project
The Great Turkey Heist
The Garden Thief
The Boardwalk Mystery
The Mystery of the Fallen Treasure
The Return of the Graveyard Ghost
The Mystery of the Stolen Snowboard
The Mystery of the Wild West Bandit
The Mystery of the Soccer Snitch

THE MYSTERY OF THE GRINNING GARGOYLE

created by
GERTRUDE CHANDLER WARNER

ALBERT WHITMAN & Company
Chicago, Illinois

Library of Congress Cataloging-in-Publication Data

Warner, Gertrude Chandler, 1890-1979.
The mystery of the grinning gargoyle / created by Gertrude Chandler Warner ;
interior illustrations by Anthony VanArsdale.
pages cm. — (The Boxcar children mysteries ; 137)
Summary: When the Aldens visit a university campus, they must solve a mystery
involving an old library whose stone gargoyles seem to move on their own.
[1. Mystery and detective stories. 2. Universities and colleges—Fiction. 3.
Gargoyles—Fiction. 4. Brothers and sisters—Fiction. 5. Orphans—Fiction.] I.
VanArsdale, Anthony, illustrator. II. Title.
PZ7.W244Mwut 2014
[Fic]—dc23
2014002088

Published in 2014 by Albert Whitman & Company.
ISBN 978-0-8075-0892-3 (hardcover)
ISBN 978-0-8075-0893-0 (paperback)

10 9 8 7 6 5 4 3 2 1 LB 19 18 17 16 15 14

Cover art by Logan Kline.
Interior illustrations by Anthony VanArsdale.

For more information about Albert Whitman & Company,
visit our web site at www.albertwhitman.com.

Contents

THE MYSTERY OF THE GRINNING GARGOYLE

CHAPTER 1

The Old Library

"Aren't the leaves lovely?" Grandfather Alden asked as he steered the car over the winding, wooded road. Autumn leaves of red, orange, and yellow covered the trees on either side.

"They sure are," said Violet Alden. "Fall is my favorite time of year."

"Those red leaves are the same color as your tie, Grandfather!" said Violet's six-year-old brother Benny.

Grandfather Alden wore that particular

necktie for a reason. As the car carrying the Alden family rounded one last curve, they saw the beautiful campus of Goldwin University, the college Grandfather had attended many years before.

Red and white were the university's colors, and could be seen on flapping red flags with white letters hanging on poles around the grassy grounds. The spirited school colors could also be seen on the red and white jackets and sweatshirts of the college students walking from building to building and playing games on the lawn. Grandfather showed his school spirit by wearing a bright white suit and a bright red tie.

"Where is the new library going to be?" asked Jessie Alden, who was twelve. She looked at the college's buildings, many of which were over a hundred years old.

"It will be where that open space is," Grandfather Alden said, pointing to an empty field. "That is where the groundbreaking will be held tomorrow morning before the big game."

"Groundbreaking?" said Benny. "Why would anyone want to break the ground?"

"It's okay, Benny," said Henry, the oldest of the Alden children. "A groundbreaking ceremony is what people do when a new building is going to be built."

"And don't worry," said Jessie, "nothing is going to be broken. All that's going to happen is a hole will be dug, just like when you dig in the sand at the beach."

Grandfather Alden parked the car in a parking lot near where Alden Library would stand. Alden Library was the reason for the family's visit. Grandfather had donated money to help build the new library. The professors and other leaders of the university were so thankful that they planned to name the building for him.

The Alden children climbed out of the car to stretch their legs and look around. Next to the empty field stood a very tall, very old building with high walls made of dark stone and high, arching windows.

"Wow!" said Benny. "Is that a castle?"

"It's not a castle," said a woman's voice, "though it looks a bit like one. This is Goldwin Library."

A tall, thin woman stood outside the doors of the old building. "James Alden," she said, "you must be here for the big ceremony." The children always found it funny to hear someone call their grandfather by his first name.

"Children," said Grandfather Alden, "this is Miss Hollenberg, the head librarian at Goldwin University. She began working at the library back when I was a student."

"And what a student your grandfather was," Miss Hollenberg said, straightening her glasses and smiling. "He spent a lot of time reading and studying in the library in order to do well in his classes."

"I only spent four years at Goldwin University, but Miss Hollenberg has spent her entire career working in this old building," said Grandfather Alden. "Because she has worked here so long, she can find information on anything a student–or anyone else–might want to learn about. And it has been her job to take care of the library."

"Of course I've had a little bit of help from the grinning gargoyles," Miss Hollenberg said.

"Gargoyles?" asked Violet. "Who are they?"

Miss Hollenberg pointed to the top of the old library building, past the arches and other decorations that covered its rock walls. There, at each corner of the roof, hunched the statue of a strange creature. Each statue had small, beady eyes, a pair of wings, long claws, and a smiling mouth full of sharp, stone teeth.

The Alden children craned their necks to look up at the statues.

"Those look like monsters!" said Benny. "Or dragons! They're kind of scary."

"They are scary looking, even if they're just stone statues," said Jessie. "But how could a statue protect the library?"

"This is a little-known fact Miss Hollenberg told me back when I was a student," Grandfather said. "As you can see from their open mouths, gargoyle statues were added to buildings to act as rain spouts—carrying rain water away like the gutters on our house. Without such protection, water would eat away at the stone."

"But some people believe that gargoyles are more than just statues," Miss Hollenberg said. "Legend has it that gargoyles guard the buildings they call home. And here at Goldwin, students have long believed that these grinning gargoyles won't be so happy if their home—the library—isn't treated right. Gargoyles are mythical creatures, of course—no such thing as a real one. But for years, troublemakers and good-for-nothings have spread rumors of running into living, breathing gargoyles. It's all balderdash, if you ask me..."

"Well, I'd like to take a closer look at the gargoyles," said Benny, "and the rest of this cool castle-looking library that they live in!"

"This library sure is cool," laughed Miss Hollenberg. "I'll surely miss it when they

tear it down—now that we'll have the new library to use. I don't see why you children can't take a look around, as long as you behave yourselves, and as long as your grandfather says yes."

"We promise to behave," Jessie said. "Can we explore the library for a bit, Grandfather?"

"Why, surely," said Grandfather Alden. "I'm already late to see an old friend at the football stadium. But when you've finished your library visit, why don't you meet me there? We can watch the Goldwin Bears practice."

The Alden children followed Mrs. Hollenberg through the tall, arched doorway. Benny looked up before walking inside and saw the gargoyles were still looking down at him, grinning.

Miss Hollenberg pointed the children to a stairway that would lead them to the top floor of the library. "You all explore," she said as she stepped behind her computer desk. "I have library work to do."

"Race you to the top!" shouted Benny,

running ahead of his brother and sisters.

"I bet we can win the race," Henry told his sisters. "Do you see that elevator?"

The other three Aldens pushed the up button on a nearby elevator panel. When the doors slid open, a library worker pushing wheeled carts of books also climbed onto the elevator. The carts were connected to each other, allowing three of them to be pushed at the same time.

"Those look like the boxcars from a train!" Violet said. Henry and Jessie laughed. Violet's comment made them think of their own boxcar back home. When the Alden children became orphans, they had run away and lived in an old boxcar in the woods. They had been afraid to live with their grandfather, fearing that he wouldn't be nice. But when they found what a kind man Grandfather Alden was, they were happy to live with him in his big house in Greenfield. As a gift, he even placed the children's boxcar in the backyard, where they used it as a playhouse.

"These are just books that have been

recently returned," said the man who worked in the library, pointing to a sign on the first cart that said "TO BE SHELVED."

The elevator slowly went up floor by floor. *Ding. Ding. Ding.* Halfway to the top, the doors opened and the library worker wheeled the cart out of the elevator.

"Maybe this elevator wasn't the fastest way of getting to the top," said Jessie.

At last the elevator doors opened at the top floor.

"Benny!" Violet called out. "We beat you!"

But there was no Benny. There were only bookshelves full of books, stretching row after row in all directions.

"Where do you think he is?" Jessie asked.

"I don't know," said Henry. "Maybe taking the stairs was even slower than that slow elevator."

"Or maybe he stopped on the way up," Violet said. "Maybe he got tired…or hungry."

"I bet you're right," said Henry. The youngest Alden was *always* hungry, though the library seemed like a better place to find a book than a snack.

Jessie looked back into the stairwell. She called her little brother's name. "Benny!" her voice echoed.

Just then, the three children heard their brother's voice echo back up the stairwell. "Oh, no!" Benny screamed. "A gargoyle is staring right at me!"

"A gargoyle?" gasped Violet.

"There's no way Benny could have seen a gargoyle," said Henry. "The gargoyles we saw from the ground were at the top of the building, on the *outside*. We're at the top of the building, not Benny. And there aren't any windows on this floor."

"Come on," said Jessie. "Let's find out what's going on."

The three ran down the stairs as quickly as they could. They dashed down the stairs to the door of the next floor. Henry reached for the doorknob, anxious to find out where his brother was calling from. The door opened onto a floor with bookshelves full of books and a large window on one wall. It also opened onto Benny because at the very same time, Benny Alden reached for the doorknob on the other side, trying to get back into the stairwell. As Benny's three siblings were about to exit the stairwell, though, their little brother bumped right into them.

"Let's get out of here!" Benny yelled as his brother and sisters collided with him. "That spooky gargoyle's staring into the library at me!"

Benny pointed at a large window just outside the stairwell door. And as the four Alden children tumbled to the floor in a heap, Henry, Jessie, and Violet caught a glimpse of something in the window.

Something that floated.

Something with beady eyes.

Something with sharp teeth.

Something with a grin on its face.

"Yikes!" said Violet, falling on top of Jessie.

"Ouch!" said Jessie, falling on top of Henry.

"Huh?" Henry said, landing on the floor with his sisters and brother tangled on top of him.

All four Aldens struggled to free themselves

from their twisted pile of arms and legs, trying to look back at the window where they all thought they'd just seen the beady-eyed, sharp-toothed, grinning face of a gargoyle!

CHAPTER 2

A New Mystery

The four Alden children untangled themselves from one another and picked themselves off the floor of the stairway landing. Then they all looked back to the large window where they'd just seen the face of a gargoyle—a grinning gargoyle just like the ones that decorated the top of the old library building.

But the window was empty. The gargoyle was nowhere to be seen.

"Did you guys see that?" Jessie asked.

"I sure did," said Violet. "It was a gargoyle."

"I saw it, too," said Henry. "But gargoyles aren't real creatures. They're just stone statues."

"But if I saw it, and you all saw it, then it must have been real," Benny said. "Right?"

"We all saw something," said Henry, "but the real questions are what exactly did we see and where did it go?"

Henry was already looking out the window—up and down and to each side—with his siblings crowded around him. "I don't see it anywhere," he said. "I wonder where it went...whatever it was that we saw."

"It couldn't have just vanished," said Violet. "Could it?"

"Tell us exactly what happened, Benny," Jessie said.

"Well," said Benny, "I was running up the stairs, and I knew I was close to the top because my legs were getting tired. I stopped to catch my breath, and that's when I heard a scratching sound. When I looked out this door to see what was scratching and scraping, there was that gargoyle, smiling right at me through the window—and it wasn't a friendly smile, either!"

"Well, like I said, gargoyles are just stone statues," said Henry. "There is no way they could fly down in front of a window, or make a scratching sound..."

Just then, there was a different sound from behind where the children stood. It was a thumping and bumping sound, and it was coming from the stairwell where the Aldens had just been.

Thump. Bump. Thump. Bump. The sound echoed all the way up to where the children were.

Benny gasped. "Could a gargoyle make that kind of sound?" he asked.

Thump. Bump. Thump. Bump.

"That sounds like someone—or something—running," said Jessie. "Who's there?"

Thump. Bump. Thump. Bump. That's the only thing the children heard.

"Yeah," Violet called down the stairs,

"who—or what—are you?"

But there was no answer, just more thumps and bumps of footsteps, from either a human or something else, running down the staircase of the old library.

"Quick!" said Henry. "Let's follow the footsteps. Maybe it's the gargoyle, or somebody who saw the gargoyle, too."

The children started to run down the stairs, but whoever or whatever they were following had too much of a head start. The thumping and bumping of the footsteps sounded farther and farther away.

Thump. Bump. Thump. Bump.

"Let's take the elevator," said Jessie. "It will be faster."

"Jessie's right," said Henry. "We got to the top floor before Benny did when he took the stairs. This is our only chance to find out who or what was behind *whatever* it was that we saw and *whoever* it is that we're hearing."

"It sounds like a mystery for us to solve!" Benny said, rushing through the door to the next floor.

As soon as the Alden children dashed out of the stairwell and onto the next floor of the library, Violet pushed the down button for the elevator. The bell dinged and the doors slid open. The children piled into the elevator and Jessie pushed the button for the ground floor.

"If we beat whoever it is to the bottom floor," said Jessie, "we can wait at the bottom of the stairwell for them."

"Good thinking!" said Henry. "That way we can see whoever it was making those noises."

"And maybe that person knows something about the spooky gargoyle we saw," said Benny.

They stood inside the elevator and watched the light for each floor light up to show how fast they were going down.

"Eight!" said Henry, calling out the floor number.

"Seven!" Jessie said as they reached the next floor.

"Six," said Violet. "We're almost halfway there!"

But instead of continuing down five more floors on its speedy trip to the library's lobby, the elevator slowed and groaned to a stop on the sixth floor. The elevator doors creaked open.

"Oh, no," said Benny. "We were so close!"

Once the doors had opened all the way, the Alden children were met by the same library worker they'd seen earlier. The man was still pushing the same connected carts of books.

"Excuse me," said the man as he pulled the carts onto the elevator. "Library books coming through. Make way for library books."

The elevator was hardly big enough for four children, a library worker, and lots of neatly stacked library books stored on carts. If the children hadn't been in such a hurry, Benny might have started talking to the library worker, asking the man's name and how he was doing and other friendly questions. But Benny just tapped his foot impatiently and under his breath told the elevator to "Hurry up!"

As Jessie was about to ask Benny to please be a little bit more polite, the elevator slowed and stopped once again.

"We're only on the third floor!" Benny said.

"This is where I get off," said the library worker. The man rolled the carts off of the elevator and told the children goodbye, not realizing what a hurry that the Alden siblings were in.

It seemed to take forever for the doors to shut once again. Benny called off the last two floors. "Two! One! We're here!"

By the time the elevator finally stopped on the first floor of the library, and by the time the doors slid open for the last time, and by the time that Henry and Jessie and Violet and Benny spilled out of the elevator and into the library lobby, there was no one in sight—no one, except for Miss Hollenberg.

"Miss Hollenberg, Miss Hollenberg!" Benny shouted, sprinting out of the open elevator. "I saw it! I saw it! And my brother and sisters did, too!"

Jessie quickly caught up with her noisy little brother, taking him by the arm. "Benny," she said, "remember that we're in a *library*...you can't just yell and run around. People are here to read and study and learn."

Sure enough, Miss Hollenberg had been working away at her computer, but looked up at the sound of running and yelling. The old librarian started to shush whoever was making the racket, and saw the Aldens coming her way.

"What's the matter, children?" she asked. "You look like you've seen a ghost."

"A gargoyle!" Benny said. "We saw the gargoyle, and it saw us!"

"Now, now," said Miss Hollenberg, "you must have seen one of the statues."

"But it wasn't one of the statues," said Violet. "The gargoyle we saw was floating outside of the window, and then it disappeared."

"And the gargoyle statues were up at the top of the roof," said Benny, "but I saw—we saw—this gargoyle on the floor right below the top floor."

"And then we heard someone or something running down the stairs," Jessie said, "but they got away because the elevator ride wasn't as fast as we thought it would be. Did you see anybody—or anything—run out of the stairwell right before we did, Miss Hollenberg?"

"I'm sorry, children. I was busy working," said Miss Hollenberg. "I didn't see anyone running around here except for the four of you."

"Now we have a new mystery to solve," said Henry. "We've solved quite a few mysteries already, and we have gotten pretty good at it, too."

Miss Hollenberg shook her head. "Children," she said, "while solving mysteries sure sounds like fun, and is probably something you're good at if you're as smart as your grandfather, you must remember that this is a library..."

"That's a great idea!" said Henry. "Miss Hollenberg, are there any old books or papers here in the library that might tell about the gargoyles? Maybe we could solve the mystery by reading about it."

"Gargoyles? Stairway chases? Mystery solving? You children certainly have good imaginations, don't you?" Miss Hollenberg chuckled. "I know this old library inside and out, and there aren't any gargoyles here, other than the statues. Like I said when you arrived—it's just a legend. And like I've already told you, please remember that this is a library. People are here to read and study, not listen to a bunch of ruckus."

"We'll be quiet," promised Jessie.

"Yeah," said Benny, "especially if you help us solve this mystery..."

"There have to be books or papers that talk about the gargoyles, don't there?" said Henry. "This library is really big and really old. I bet there are books and papers about *everything* in here."

"Well, there are thousands and thousands of books in this old building," said Miss Hollenberg. "And nearly as many old papers and documents. But I can assure you children that there aren't any clues about gargoyles hidden in books or papers, so don't bother looking.

Henry thought that was not a very librarian-like thing for Miss Hollenberg to say. Most every librarian he had ever met—and since Henry loved books, he'd met quite a few—loved when children wanted to read old books and learn new things. Miss Hollenberg was acting strange.

The old librarian continued talking. "Now, I clearly remember hearing your grandfather tell you to meet him at the football field," she said. "That would be a much better place for such loud and rambunctious behavior, don't you think?"

***

As the Aldens trudged across the campus of Goldwin University to the football stadium, they were a little discouraged.

"I wish we could have stayed at the library," said Henry. "There must have been clues we missed that would have solved the gargoyle mystery. I'm sure that the gargoyles aren't real, and that someone is just trying to scare people."

"I wish Miss Hollenberg had listened to us," said Violet. "Maybe she could have helped us solve the mystery, since she knows so much about the library."

"I wish that elevator had been a little bit faster," said Jessie. "We could have solved the mystery if we had made it downstairs a little sooner."

"And I wish," said Benny, "that we had something to eat. I'm hungry!"

Benny was always hungry, and the scare and chase he'd had at the library made his stomach growl even louder than usual.

"The Bruin Beanery," said Jessie, pointing at a shop ahead of them on the sidewalk. "Maybe there's something to eat there."

"What's a bruin?" Violet asked. "And what's a beanery?"

"Bruin is just another word for bear," Henry said. "The mascot of Goldwin University is a bear, or a bruin."

"And beanery is another way to say coffee

shop," said Jessie. "Most coffee shops also have food for sale..."

Before Jessie could finish her thought, Benny's nose had already caught the scent of something tasty. The youngest Alden ran down the sidewalk and through the front door of the Bruin Beanery, yelling, "I smell chocolate chip cookies!"

Benny's siblings reached the counter of the coffee shop and found their brother already ordering from the clerk.

"I'd like four chocolate chip cookies, please," Benny said to the clerk behind the counter.

The clerk was a gloomy-looking college student dressed in black. Her hair was jet black, too, and she wore black eyeliner around her eyes. The Bruin Beanery badge on her chest said that her name was Raven. "Four chocolate chip cookies for the four of you?" the girl asked.

"No," said Benny. "The cookies are for me. I'm really hungry!"

With their afternoon snacks sitting on a

table in the middle of the coffee shop, the Alden children sat down on tall stools. Henry had ordered a bagel with cream cheese. Jessie munched on a slice of zucchini bread. Violet had a blueberry muffin, with juicy, purple berries oozing through her fingers.

"These cookies sure are great," Benny said kind of loudly. "They almost made me forget about that scary gargoyle I saw."

"What did you say?" asked Raven the coffee-shop clerk from across the shop.

"I said these cookies are delicious," said Benny. "Did you make them yourself?"

"No," said Raven. "What did you say about a gargoyle?"

"My little brother Benny saw a gargoyle at the library," said Jessie.

"Actually, we all saw it," said Violet.

"You saw a gargoyle?" Raven asked. She didn't look so gloomy anymore. Instead, she looked very excited and rushed out from behind the cash register, coming over to the children's table. "Tell me about it."

Henry told Raven all about the gargoyle

Benny had seen, about how it disappeared, and about the slow elevator ride to the first floor of the library as they chased the source of the mysterious thumping and bumping sound they had heard echoing up the stairwell. "Why are you so interested in the gargoyles?" Henry asked. "Have you seen one before?"

"Yes, I have," said Raven. "I've been gargoyle hunting for the past month. For years there has been a legend of the grinning gargoyle, but ever since the new library was announced, a gargoyle has actually started appearing around town and scaring people. And once people started seeing it, I decided to catch the gargoyle on video. I've actually spotted it quite a few times. My online gargoyle videos are very popular. I have thousands of hits so far."

"Well, we don't think the gargoyle is a real creature," said Henry. " Gargoyles are just statues made of stone. But we did see *something* up there in the library. It's a mystery! And the four of us plan on solving this mystery."

RAVEN

"Let me know if you see it," said Raven. "And be sure to check out my online videos!"

Jessie pointed at the clock on the coffee shop wall. "We'd better meet Grandfather at the football stadium," she said.

"Thank you for the cookies!" Benny said.

"And thank you for the information," said Henry. "We'll let you know if we find anything."

"You can find me online," said Raven, "or in my dorm, Harper Hall. I live in room 4B."

After saying goodbye to Raven, the Aldens walked the rest of the way across campus, discussing everything that they had seen and heard so far.

"Raven sure seems interested in the grinning gargoyle," said Henry.

"And she sure seems proud of her videos," said Jessie, "and how many people have watched them. Do you think she might be behind the gargoyles that people are seeing."

"Or the gargoyle that we saw?" said Benny.

"Remember, Benny," said Jessie, "that gargoyle wasn't real. Someone was behind it, and Raven seems like she could have been that someone. I think we should keep her in mind as we try to solve this mystery."

The children soon reached the football field. The stadium was a building that looked as ancient as the library. It was made of old, dark stone and had soaring arches all around its curved walls. Above the tall arch over the entrance were the words *Goldwin Coliseum.*

"Coliseum," said Henry. "That's the name of a giant outdoor stadium in Italy where the ancient Romans used to hold games and events. I read about it in school, and saw pictures of it in my history book. The Goldwin Coliseum looks almost as old as the Roman one!"

Henry led the way as the Aldens entered Goldwin Coliseum and made their way through tunnels and walkways until they heard the sounds of football practice. The children scurried down the concrete stairs past row after row of red, metal bleachers once they saw Grandfather Alden waving at them from the fifty-yard line of the football field.

"Grandfather," said Benny as he reached the green grass that was lined with white lines and marks, "you won't believe what we saw!"

"I can't wait to hear about it," Grandfather said, "but first let me introduce you to Goldwin University's famous football coach. This is Coach Woods. Back when I was a student here, he was our star player and a very close friend of mine. But now he coaches the Bears to victory every football season."

A stocky older man stood next to Grandfather. He wore a red cap and jacket and had a shiny, silver whistle around his neck. Coach Woods shook each of the Alden children's hands with a big, strong grip, saying, "James has told me all about you children. He's very proud of you."

Then the coach pointed to the players on the field, tossed a football to the children, and said, "Why don't you kids run out there and show me what you've got?"

CHAPTER 3

Nice Catch

The Aldens were big football fans. The children loved to sit with Grandfather and cheer for the Goldwin Bears each week when the team played on television. They also loved to throw and catch the football in their big backyard in Greenfield. So the chance to run around a real football field was too good to pass up. It even made the four children forget about their latest mystery for a minute or two.

"This is great being on the same field as the

guys we see on TV!" said Violet, staring at the big, strong players in their red uniforms and white helmets.

"But the field doesn't look quite like it does on TV," Jessie said.

Jessie was right. The field of Goldwin Coliseum didn't seem as big as it did on television. It didn't seem as fancy as other sports arenas the Alden children had seen or visited, either. The cement steps they had run down had been chipped and crumbling. The seats were hard metal bleachers, and not the cushioned chairs that some stadiums had. And the grass on the field was brown in some places, with patches of dirt and holes in other spots. But a football field was a football field, and they had the chance to play some football.

"Benny, run out and try to catch it!" said Henry.

Henry threw the football as far as he could and Benny sprinted down the field. The ball looked like it was going to fly far over his head, but at the last second Benny dove. He tumbled head-over-heels, and when he came to a stop, Benny held the football tightly in his hands.

"Nice catch!" Jessie said to her younger brother.

Benny stood up, dusting the white chalk from the football field off of his arms and legs. Then he proudly carried the football back to his siblings.

"Look up there, Benny," said Violet. "You're on the big video screen!"

Benny looked up at the screen that showed replays for the fans at football games, and watched himself dive for the football and catch it. The video of Benny's nice catch played again and again, causing his siblings, his grandfather, and all of the Goldwin football team players to erupt in cheers.

"You're quite a receiver!" Coach Woods called from the sideline. "When you get older, maybe you'll be a Goldwin Bear, too."

Once the giant screen went blank, the four children watched the actual Goldwin Bears practice running and throwing and kicking and catching. The players were all very fast and very strong. Benny hoped one day he'd be as good at football as they were.

But one of the players was even faster and stronger than the rest of his teammates. The player with number 44 on the back of his red jersey could run like the wind. None of the other players could catch him, and if they did catch him, they couldn't tackle him. When the quarterback threw him a pass, Number 44 always seemed to catch it. Catch after catch, Number 44 never let the football touch the ground.

Then, as Number 44 leaped into the air to grab the football, he landed with a crunch.

"Ouch!" he said, falling to the ground. "I think I hurt my leg."

The Alden children made it to the hurt player first.

"Are you okay?" Jessie asked. "Where does it hurt?"

"What happened?" asked Benny.

Number 44 lay on his back, holding his leg. "When I jumped up to catch the ball, my

44

foot landed in one of those holes in the field. I must have twisted my ankle in the hole."

A man with a first-aid kit ran over from the sidelines, Coach Woods jogging right behind him.

"It looks like he hurt his foot or leg," Henry said.

"It will be okay, children," the man said. "I'm the team's trainer. I take care of any players who get hurt. This looks like it's only a slightly sprained ankle."

Coach Woods knelt on the ground looking unhappy. "We can't afford to lose you right before the big game," said the coach.

The trainer pulled a heavy bandage from his kit and wrapped the player's ankle. Then Coach Woods wiped white dust from his hands and helped the player stand up. Number 44 leaned on the two men and limped off the field.

As the player, coach, and trainer passed by, the Alden children heard Coach Woods mumbling under his breath.

"I've been telling them we need a new

stadium for years," said the coach. "Now look—our star player is hurt the day before the big game, and it's because the field is in such poor shape. Why, Goldwin Coliseum is even older than the library. The only nice thing about it is that fancy video screen. Shouldn't they build a new football stadium before they build a new library? Shouldn't they just leave the old library alone? Maybe those gosh-darn gargoyles are onto something!"

The children weren't the only ones to hear what Coach Woods had said. Grandfather Alden had, too.

"Coach," said Grandfather, "I didn't realize that the old stadium had fallen into such bad shape. If I had, I might have done something to help out."

"That's the problem," Coach Woods said. "Everyone's so excited to cheer for the team and so excited that we usually win that they don't pay any attention to how old the stadium we play in is. It's almost like I'm one of those old gargoyles, always there for the university, and everyone takes me for granted."

"I'm sorry you feel that way," Grandfather Alden said. "Maybe there's something I could do to help. Maybe I could get the word out."

"Maybe the gargoyles could get the word out." said Coach Woods.

"What?" Grandfather Alden asked.

"Oh, nothing," said Coach Woods. "My team has a game for me to coach, so I'd better just forget about this lousy old stadium."

"Did you hear that?" Violet asked her siblings once they were away from the football team. "He was talking about the gargoyles."

"Nice catch, Violet!" said Henry. "It sounds like Coach Woods doesn't want anyone messing with the old library. We'd better remember that as we try to solve this mystery."

"Mystery? Are you children on the case of another mystery?" It was Grandfather Alden, having left Coach Woods's side to catch up with his grandchildren. He knew that they were very good at solving mysteries, and was very proud of their detective skills.

"Yes, Grandfather," said Violet. "We're investigating the case of the grinning gargoyles."

"You heard Miss Hollenberg tell us about the legend of the gargoyles, didn't you?" Jessie asked.

"I certainly did," said Grandfather Alden.

"When I was running up the stairs at the library, I saw a gargoyle!" Benny said.

"We all saw it," said Jessie.

"We all saw *something*," said Henry, "since gargoyles are just stone statues and can't actually fly down from the roof and scare people. It must be someone making everyone think the gargoyle legend is true, and we're going to figure out who it is!"

"Well, maybe we should get some dinner," Grandfather Alden said. "Detective work is always more productive on a full stomach."

"Dinner sounds great," said Benny. "Playing football and playing detective both make me really hungry!"

"I know just the place," said Grandfather Alden. "We'll eat at what was my favorite restaurant when I was a student."

The Aldens said goodbye to the football team and Coach Woods, then climbed the old gray steps of Goldwin Coliseum. The five of them laughed and talked as they crossed the college campus, admiring the beautiful autumn leaves that fell from the trees.

Soon they came to an old wooden building with a sign that said Goldwin Gyros.

"It might not look like much," said Grandfather Alden, "but Goldwin Gyros serves the tastiest food on campus."

Grandfather held the door for his grandchildren and, of course, Benny was the first one into the restaurant. But no sooner had Benny dashed inside, he yelled and turned around.

"You guys have to see this!" he said, pointing. Standing there was a big, bald man with a big, bushy, black mustache and a big, bright smile. He looked friendly, so Benny shouldn't have been alarmed.

But the big sign the man held didn't look so friendly. On it was painted a sharp-toothed, smiling creature with wings—a gargoyle! The sign read "BITE INTO A GARGOYLE GYRO!"

The Alden children looked past the sign and around the main dining room of Goldwin Gyros. Painted on the walls were other gargoyles, peering down at the customers with toothy grins. There were gargoyles over each table and booth. There were gargoyles over the counter and underneath the cash register. There were even gargoyles painted onto the restroom doors—one wearing a skirt for the girls' room, and one without a skirt for the boys'.

And on the t-shirt that the bald man wore under his white, dusty apron was yet another gargoyle and the words, "DON'T LET THE GARGOYLE GET YOU!"

While Benny peeked out from behind Grandfather Alden's back, Henry, Jessie, and Violet looked at one another. All four children watched as the man stepped toward them and said, "Welcome, Alden family. I'm so glad you dropped by!"

"Where are all the customers?" Violet whispered to Jessie.

"Maybe they were scared off by all of the gargoyles," Benny whispered.

"This place is a little bit spooky, being so empty," Jessie whispered.

"Maybe we should keep our eyes peeled for clues," whispered Henry, trying not to be heard as the bald man surrounded by all of those gargoyles welcomed the family into the empty, spooky place.

CHAPTER 4

The Gargoyle Gyro

"Izzy!" Grandfather Alden said to the mustached man in the apron. "It's so good to see you again."

"James Alden," said the man, wiping what looked like white flour from his hands before patting the children's grandfather on the back, "it has been years since you've eaten here."

"Children," Grandfather Alden said, "I'd like you to meet Izzy. His father owns the restaurant. Izzy was a student at Goldwin

University at the same time I was. He studied art here, and is one of the best artists I have ever seen. He can draw, paint, or sculpt beautiful art pieces."

"I might know a thing or two about art," said the man, "but I was never the student that your grandfather was. I spent more time with a paintbrush than I ever did in the library. Now let's get you all something to eat."

"You must have been baking something good," said Jessie, who did much of the cooking and baking for her family. "That's flour all over your hands, right?"

Izzy wiped his hands a bit more. "Yes, yes," he said nervously, "that's *flour* on my hands. I've been baking bread, *of course!*"

Since Benny loved eating so much, he knew the smell of baking bread. "Mmmm!" he said. "I can smell garlic and cucumbers and roasting meat! But I can't smell any baked bread."

"Oh, that's right," said Izzy, "my bread oven isn't working, so I had to buy today's pita and other baked goods from a bakery.

Yeah, that's what happened."

Henry and Jessie looked at one another. Something seemed strange with Izzy's story.

But all was forgotten for a moment when Izzy showed the Aldens to a table, where they sat down and began to look through the restaurant's menu. Everything on the menu looked and sounded delicious.

"Where is your father?" Grandfather Alden asked Izzy. "He always made the best food."

"My father retired a month ago and moved to Florida, where the weather is warmer," said Izzy. "Now I'm running Goldwin Gyros. I'd be honored if you would try our latest and greatest specialty—the Gargoyle Gyro!"

Benny's eyes grew big when he heard the word gargoyle yet again. But they grew even bigger when he saw that particular item on the menu. "That looks good! But, wait, what's a ji-ro?" he said, pronouncing the name of the food all wrong.

"It's called a *year-ro*," said Izzy, "pronounced to rhyme with 'hero.' And it's a

Greek sandwich. Sliced and roasted meat is wrapped up with vegetables like tomatoes and onions inside a freshly baked piece of pita bread. Then I slather the whole thing with creamy cucumber sauce. My gyros have always been the biggest and best in town. But the Gargoyle Gyro is even bigger and better!"

"The Gargoyle Gyro is huge!" Benny said, pronouncing the word right and pointing to the picture of a gigantic gyro sandwich. "But I bet I can finish the whole thing. I'll take one Gargoyle Gyro, please, Mr. Izzy."

Benny's family also decided what they wanted for dinner, and Izzy hurried their order to the kitchen in back.

"There sure are a lot of gargoyles in this place," Violet whispered to Jessie.

"Violet's right," Jessie whispered to Henry. "After what we saw earlier, all of these gargoyles are a little bit creepy."

"Maybe Izzy just really likes gargoyles," Henry said. "And maybe he can help us with our gargoyle mystery. Let's ask him when he comes back."

When Izzy came back out carrying a tray with five plates of piping hot food, he sat down with the Aldens and began to catch up with Grandfather.

"This is the same thing I ordered when I was a young man," said Grandfather, biting into a juicy hamburger and washing it down with a thick vanilla milkshake.

Henry had a grilled cheese sandwich and a bowl of cheesy broccoli soup. Jessie ate a Greek salad with crisp, green lettuce and chunks of salty feta cheese. Violet took a bite of the delicious fried eggplant sandwich that she had ordered, wiping the tangy tomato sauce from the corners of her mouth.

"This Gargoyle Gyro is great!" said Benny. He had sauce all around his mouth, too—the creamy cucumber sauce that covered the tasty gyro meat and enormous pita filling his plate.

"We all agree," Grandfather Alden smiled. "Goldwin Gyros is still the best restaurant on campus!"

"I still use all of my father's recipes," Izzy

said. "But as you can see, I've made some changes to the restaurant."

"It doesn't look much different from when we were students and would stop by to have burgers and shakes," said Grandfather Alden. "Except for the gargoyles, of course."

"Why are there so many gargoyles everywhere?" Benny asked.

Izzy laughed. "After my father retired, business slowed down at the restaurant. I think people were used to the way he made the food. But then, with all of the gargoyle craziness going on around campus, I decided to turn it into something fun. That's how I came up with the idea for the Gargoyle Gyro. And now that students are talking about gargoyles and even making online movies about gargoyles, Gargoyle Gyros are selling like hotcakes—or gyros!"

"I'm sure glad you did, Mr. Izzy," said Benny. "But I still don't like actual gargoyles. Especially not after I saw one staring at me today!"

Benny and his siblings told Izzy about what

they had seen, and about chasing the noise down the library stairs.

"Close call!" Izzy said, wiping sweat from his bald head and twirling his mustache. "It sounds like you almost caught yourselves a gargoyle."

"But gargoyles aren't real," said Jessie.

"You don't believe in the legend of the grinning gargoyles?" Izzy asked.

"No," said Henry. "That's all it is—a legend. And Miss Hollenberg the librarian even said there was no such thing…"

"Yeah," said Benny, "Miss Hollenberg even called it 'boulder trash' when we told her about what we saw."

"It's 'balderdash,'" Henry laughed. "She called it 'balderdash,' which is another word for nonsense. Miss Hollenberg didn't seem to think that the legend was true."

"I'm not so sure that the gargoyles *are* nonsense, though," said Izzy.

"Why do you say that?" Henry asked. "Have you ever seen one?"

"I haven't seen any gargoyles, other than

those beautiful sculptures at the top of the old library," Izzy said. "But I have read about the legend—at the library."

"Where did you read about it?" asked Jessie. "Miss Hollenberg said there weren't any books or papers about the gargoyles in the library."

"I didn't read about it in a book or a paper," said Izzy. "I read about it online. I was at the library, using the computers there to research old articles about my father's restaurant. While scrolling through the old issues of the college newspaper, *The Goldwin Gazette*, online, I found an article published about the gargoyles."

"What did the article say?" Henry asked.

"It talked about how the gargoyles protect the library," Izzy said. "Maybe now that the new Alden Library is being built to replace the old library, the gargoyles are angry."

Grandfather Alden laughed. "You're still quite a joker, Izzy. I bet even the gargoyles—if they *were* real—would appreciate the new library I'm helping Goldwin University build. Change isn't a bad thing. Why, your restaurant has changed from when we were students, but it's still the best one around."

"I agree with that," Benny said as he swallowed the last of his Gargoyle Gyro. "See, I told you I could eat the whole thing!"

The rest of the Aldens had finished their dinner, too, and it was time to say goodbye to Izzy and Goldwin Gyros.

"Should we head to the rooms at my old dormitory where we'll be staying?" Grandfather Alden asked his grandchildren. "I'm tired from the drive and the long day."

"You go ahead and get some rest, Grandfather," said Jessie. "We're going to head to the library first to check a couple of things. We'll meet you at the dorm once we're done."

"Okay," said Grandfather. "We'll be staying at Harper Hall, in Suite 4A. Good night, Izzy. We'll see you at the groundbreaking ceremony tomorrow, won't we?"

"I'm sure you will," Izzy said.

The sun had already set as the Alden

children reached the library. The moon was full and its light shined behind the old building, making it look especially spooky. The moonlight danced off the grinning faces of the gargoyles, making their teeth gleam in the night.

But the moon wasn't the only shining light the Aldens saw.

"Look!" said Violet, pointing to the top floor of the library. "There's a light on up there."

"That's near where I saw the gargoyle," Benny said.

"We'll check the light out," said Henry, "just as soon as we look into a couple of other things that I want to clear up."

CHAPTER 5

Online Sleuths

The library was still open, even that late on a Friday night.

"It's pretty late for the library to be open, isn't it?" Violet asked. "The library back home in Greenfield closes at four, right?"

"The Greenfield library closes at five," Henry said. "But a university library is a bit different. College students study at all hours of the day—even at night, and even on the weekend!"

But although the building was open, as

the Alden children went inside, they found it empty compared to their earlier visit.

"It's so quiet in here," Benny whispered. "Even for a library."

"We should probably ask Miss Hollenberg if it's okay for us to be here," Jessie said.

But Miss Hollenberg wasn't at her desk, and her computer screen was dark. There were other computers still running, though, and that is exactly what Henry wanted to see.

"Before we go searching the library building for clues," Henry said, "I want to search online."

"Let's leave Miss Hollenberg a note first," Jessie said, "just to let her know that we're here and that we won't act up."

Jessie took a blank sheet of paper from Miss Hollenberg's desk and picked up a blue pen—her favorite color. As she started to write the note, she noticed a yellowed newspaper on the desk, sticking out from under a pile of other papers. The part of the newspaper that showed had a picture of a gargoyle on it.

"Wow!" Benny said, reaching for the

newspaper. "A gargoyle!"

But Jessie stopped her brother. "This isn't our desk. Maybe tomorrow we can ask Miss Hollenberg if we can see the newspaper."

The children left the note, then left the desk. They pulled up four chairs to a table that held a computer that was turned on.

"What are we looking for?" Violet asked.

"First, I think we should find the old newspaper article that Izzy mentioned," said Henry.

"And don't forget the online videos that Raven at the Bruin Beanery told us to watch," Jessie added.

Henry typed in GARGOYLE and LIBRARY and GOLDWIN GAZETTE, then he hit "search." In less than a second, a link to the article Izzy mentioned popped up on the computer screen.

Henry clicked the link. "This article is almost fifty years old!" he said. Then the four of them read the article that was on the screen.

Gargoyles Protect Goldwin from Good-for-Nothings

By Holly Page

Students attend college in order to learn. While at college, students go to the library to quietly study so that they can do well in their classes and learn new things.

But lately here at Goldwin University, the library has not been very quiet. Good-for-nothings have been coming to the library to make noise and cause trouble. They think the library is a place to have rowdy fun.

But these troublemakers should beware. Legend has it that the grinning gargoyles that live atop the library building do not like people who don't respect their home. According to this legend, if the gargoyles become angry, they will fly down from the library roof, scratch on your windows, and scare you.

So respect Goldwin University's fair library, or face the grinning gargoyles!

"Izzy was right," said Benny. "There is a legend of the grinning gargoyles."

"And look at the picture," said Violet, pointing at the computer screen. "That's the same picture that's on the newspaper on Miss Hollenberg's desk."

"Why would she tell us that we wouldn't find any clues here in the library?" Henry asked. "Do you think she might be behind the gargoyles?"

"She seems very nice," said Jessie, "but she also might be sad about the Alden Library replacing this old library. Maybe she's trying to protect it, just like the gargoyles in the legend. She could be a good suspect. But first, let's look at Raven's videos."

Henry did another search on the computer and soon found several videos Raven had made about the gargoyles at Goldwin University. He clicked the first video and the children began to watch.

On the video, a girl stood in a dark stairwell, dressed all in black and looking as gloomy as she had looked at the coffee shop.

"That's Raven!" said Benny. "That's the girl who sold me those yummy cookies! And she's on a movie! In the same stairwell we went running down!"

"Here I am, in the old library," Raven said to the camera. "I'm hunting for the eerie and elusive Goldwin grinning gargoyle."

There was a scratching from somewhere off camera—a scary, scratchy scratching, like claws on a wall or a window. But Raven didn't look scared.

"I hear something," Raven told the camera. "I think it might be a gargoyle!"

Slowly, Raven opened the door of the stairway. The camera didn't show what was behind the door, though. It only showed Raven's face.

"Oh, no!" said Raven. "It's a gargoyle! But I'm not afraid. I've got you, gargoyle!"

The camera followed Raven as she ran from the door to the window. When it finally turned to film what Raven had seen, the window was empty.

"Once again, the grinning gargoyle of

Goldwin University away before I could catch it on camera," said Raven. "But keep watching my online videos—soon enough I'm going to film the ghoulish, grinning gargoyle, and you, my computer fans, will be the first to see it!"

The Alden children turned away from the computer screen and toward one another.

"Raven sure seems worried about getting people to watch her videos," said Jessie.

"But her video didn't show the gargoyle," said Henry. "If she was behind it, wouldn't she want to show what it looks like?"

"Not if she wants her fans to keep coming back," Jessie said. "I think she's another good suspect."

"This is kind of boring," Benny said. "I thought we were going to look for some real clues."

"These *are* real clues," Henry said. "But you're right. We can go look around the library now and see if there's anything we missed."

The library wasn't just quieter when it was

nearly empty at night—it was spookier, too. Now, the Alden children didn't believe that ghosts or ghouls or gargoyles were real, but they were all a little shy about climbing the empty, echo-y stairs when it was so late and they were so alone. So they decided to take the elevator.

Benny rushed to be the one to push the up button. His siblings waited with him while the elevator came down to the first floor. While they stood there, they noticed more carts of books waiting there, too.

Violet read the titles of the books out loud. "*Pablo Picasso*, *Painting with Watercolors*, *Papier-mâché*," she read excitedly. "Those books are all about my favorite thing—art!"

"You're right, Violet," Henry said. "Pablo Picasso was a famous painter. Papier-mâché is a type of craft where gluey strips of paper are formed into shapes and allowed to harden. It's how piñatas are made."

"And these books are arranged in alphabetical order," said Jessie, "waiting to be put on the library's bookshelves so people can find them and check them out."

At last, the elevator arrived. It carried the children to the floor where they had seen the gargoyle.

The four of them studied the window where the gargoyle had been. They looked all around it, and all around the rest of the room. But there were no clues to be found.

"What about the light we saw on the top floor?" Violet asked.

"Let's take a look," said Henry. "We never got a chance to look around up there, since we ran downstairs when Benny screamed."

The top floor was hardly lit, and a little bit spooky. The Alden children made their way through aisles of books and around dark corners.

"Look at these books!" Henry said suddenly. "They're college yearbooks from a long time ago. I bet we could find who that Holly Page was who wrote about the gargoyle legend. Everyone grab a book and check the index!"

The Aldens looked in the back of each

yearbook, searching the indexes for the name "Holly Page." The name was nowhere to be found.

Then the four of them flipped through page after page of black-and-white photographs of students from decades before. Soon they had searched all of the old, dusty college yearbooks. But after looking at all of those pages of pictures, they still found no Holly Page.

"That's strange," said Jessie. "It's almost like Holly Page wasn't a real person."

The children continued their search of the library's top floor. As they rounded yet another dark corner of what seemed to be an entire floor without windows, they came to the window where they'd seen the light—a window that looked outside. And outside that window, they could see one of the stone gargoyles.

"Look!" said Violet. "It's a gargoyle! It scared me until I realized it's just one of the statues."

"And look at this!" Jessie said, wiping her

fingers across the windowsill. “There’s some kind of white powder here.”

Henry bent down and picked up a piece of string off the floor underneath the window. “What about this? Maybe this string and the powder are clues…”

But their findings were cut short by a sound coming from somewhere nearby.

“Do you hear that scratching sound?” she asked.

Henry, Violet, and Benny all nodded that they heard it, too.

Scratch.

Scratch.

Scratch.

CHAPTER 6

Scratch, Scratch, Scream

"Where is the scratching coming from?" Violet asked.

"Is it a gargoyle?" Benny wondered.

"It's coming from over here," Henry said. "Follow me."

The children walked down a short hallway. The scratching grew louder.

They turned a corner, and came to another room where another stone gargoyle could be seen from a window. But the gargoyle outside the window wasn't scratching. It was the person in the room who was making the scratching sound.

It was Coach Woods, and he was writing on a chalkboard.

"Coach Woods," Henry said. "What are you doing here?"

The coach turned around, surprised to see— "I guess I could ask you four the same question," he said. "I'm just up here getting ready for tomorrow's big game."

On the chalkboard were all sorts of X's and O's. Coach Woods was drawing the letters and then connecting them or moving them with lines and squiggles.

"How will all those scribbles and letters help your football team?" Benny asked.

Coach Woods laughed. "What I am doing is drawing up plays," he said. "Each of these X's and each of these O's is a player. And the different directions I am making them move shows where I want the players to go. Watch this..."

The coach drew a straight line from an O, making it stretch the length of the chalkboard. "Pretend this is you, Benny," he said.

"This is the quarterback," said Coach Woods, pointing at another O. "He's the one who throws the football."

Then the coach drew a dotted line from that O to the O that was Benny. "And that dotted line is the football. See? You just caught a touchdown pass. Way to go, Benny Alden!"

"I like that idea!" said Benny. "But all of that still looks like scribbles to me."

"I never was much of an artist," said Coach Woods. "But I do know about football."

"Why are you drawing your football plays here in the library?" Henry asked. "Isn't there a place to draw them at Goldwin Coliseum?"

"Yeah," said Benny. "Aren't you afraid of the grinning gargoyles?"

"I have to come here," said the coach, "because there has been a flood in the room of the stadium where I usually draw my football plays. The plumbing at Goldwin Coliseum is so old and rusty that some of the pipes have burst. So unless I want to stand in a yard of water, there's no way for me to plan a fifty-yard football play.

"And about these gargoyles," Coach Woods said, pointing to the statue outside of the window, "I'm not afraid of them at all. In fact, sometimes it seems like they're the only ones who agree with me that this old library should stay."

"I'm not afraid of the gargoyles, either," said Benny.

"You're not only a very good football player, but you're brave, too!" said Coach Woods. "Now, children, I had better get back to my chalkboard so that we can win tomorrow. As you saw, our star player might not be able to play, so I have my work cut out for me."

"We have some work to do, too," said Henry. "Good luck tomorrow!"

The Alden children left Coach Woods to his football plays, and left the library for the night. They'd already spent more time there than they had planned, and their grandfather might be wondering where they were.

Hurrying across campus, the children looked back at the old library. In the moonlight, the old building looked kind of like a scary old castle, and its gargoyles stood out like shadows, lurking from its roof and looking down on whoever might try to uncover their secrets. The Aldens hurried even faster, and soon reached Harper Hall, where they would spend the night.

Finding the door that said 4A, the children quietly entered their suite of rooms, in case Grandfather Alden was already asleep. Even with his door closed, their grandfather's snoring told the children that he was.

The suite had a large main room with two couches and two chairs. Besides Grandfather's closed door, there were two other bedrooms connected to the living room. Benny and Henry saw that Grandfather had already placed their duffel bags in one bedroom, while Violet and Jessie found their bags in another.

"Before we all go to bed, maybe we should go over what we learned today," said Jessie.

"Let's sit out here and talk. Grandfather is such a sound sleeper that we won't wake him.

"Good idea," Henry said, plopping down onto one of the couches while his siblings sat down next to him. "Who are our suspects so far?"

"I'll go first," said Jessie. "I think Raven is a very good suspect. She really seems interested in the gargoyles *and* interested in getting attention. Maybe she's somehow faking the gargoyle sightings so that people will like her and her videos."

"Izzy seems really interested in gargoyles, too," said Violet. "Remember all of the gargoyles painted all over the walls of Goldwin Gyros? They were even on the washrooms! And remember the Gargoyle Gyro?"

"I remember the Gargoyle Gyro!" said Benny, rubbing his stomach. "I could eat another one right now."

"It's a little late for that, Benny," Jessie said. "But can you think of any suspects who might be behind the grinning gargoyle that you saw?"

"I think it might be Miss Hollenberg," Benny said. "She didn't want us snooping around the library, and she had that spooky gargoyle newspaper on her desk."

"Good thinking, Benny," said Henry. "But I think Coach Woods could be behind the gargoyle sightings."

"Coach Woods?" Benny asked. "But he's so nice. He said I was brave, and really good at football. He even tried to draw me on his chalkboard."

"That's just it," Henry said. "Don't you remember that Coach Woods wants a brand new stadium to be built instead of a new library? What if he's pretending the gargoyles are trying to protect the old library, so that a new one can't be built?"

"We have four good suspects," said Jessie. "I think we should look at all of them first thing tomorrow morning."

"Jessie," Benny interrupted, "do you hear that?"

The children listened closely. They all heard it.

More scratching.

Scratch.

Scratch.

Scratch.

"It's coming from the room where Jessie and Violet will be sleeping," said Henry. "Quick! Let's check it out."

By the time the children had reached the girls' room, the bedroom window was empty and the scratching had stopped.

But then the scratching started again.

This time it was coming from another room.

"That sounds like the room where we're going to sleep, Henry," Benny said.

The children left the girls' room and followed the scratching into the boys'.

But again, they weren't quick enough.

"There's nothing outside this window, either," said Jessie.

"And I don't hear the scratching anymore," said Violet.

Violet was right. The four children heard nothing.

There was nothing but silence, and the snores coming from Grandfather Alden's bedroom.

Then another sound drowned out the silence and the snores.

But this sound wasn't a scratch, scratch, scratch.

This sound was a SCREAM!

"Aaaaahhhh!"

The scream was followed by another scream and another.

"Aaaaahhhh! Aaaaahhhh! Aaaaahhhh!"

The Alden children ran into the living room, but the screaming wasn't coming from there, either. The screams were not coming from anywhere inside the family's suite, but they were loud and clear.

"Aaaaahhhh!"

And it was clear that whoever was screaming so loud was scared and could use the Aldens' help.

4B

CHAPTER 7

An Unsuspecting Suspect

The Alden children dashed out the door of their suite and ran down the dorm hallway, following the sound of the scream. They didn't have far to go.

The screaming was coming from the door marked 4B.

"Wait a second," Jessie said. "Didn't Raven tell us that she lived in room 4B? Maybe this is some kind of act for her online videos."

"Those screams sound pretty real to me," said Henry. He knocked on the door and called, “Raven, are you in there? Are you okay?”

The screaming stopped. From inside the room a quivering voice asked, “Wh-wh-who’s there?”

“It’s the Alden children,” Henry said. “Henry, Jessie, Violet, and Benny. We heard screaming, and came to make sure everything was okay.”

The door to 4B opened a crack. A very frightened college student peeked out. Tears streamed down her face. But this wasn’t a girl in black with black hair. This girl’s hair was light brown and she wore pink pajamas with cupcakes on them. The girl tightly clutched a purple teddy bear to her chest.

“It was a gargoyle,” said the girl, opening the door and letting the Aldens come into the dorm room. “I saw it outside of my window.”

Violet put an arm around the girl and said, “I like your teddy bear. Purple is my favorite color.”

“And I like your pajamas,” Benny said. “Those cupcakes look really yummy!”

"Thanks," the girl said, wiping tears from her eyes.

"You saw a gargoyle?" Henry asked. "There's nothing in the window."

"The gargoyle was floating right there, grinning at me." The girl pointed at her window. "I swear that I saw it. But it disappeared when you knocked on my door."

"Where is Raven?" asked Jessie. "She told us that 4B was her dorm room. Do you think she's trying to scare you to make another one of her videos about the grinning gargoyles here at Goldwin University?"

"I'm Raven," the girl said in a very quiet voice. "At least I am sometimes."

The girl opened her closet and pointed to a row of black clothing hanging on hangers. Also hanging in the closet was a jet-black wig—the same hair the children had seen on Raven's head while she worked at the Bruin Beanery. Sitting on a shelf by a mirror was a jar of black eyeliner. The rest of the room wasn't so black and gloomy, though. Next to the black clothes hung pink and purple shirts and pairs of blue jeans. Hanging on the walls were pictures of horses and dolphins. Covering the dorm room's bed was a comforter decorated with hot-air balloons.

"I'm confused," said Benny. "Raven isn't real? But she gave me those delicious chocolate chip cookies."

The girl stopped looking scared for a second and smiled a very small smile. "I gave you those cookies, Benny. Like I said, I *am* Raven. At least I play her on the videos, and I dress up like her when I leave my dorm room."

"So if those black clothes and black hair are just a costume you dress up in," Violet said, "who are you in real life?"

"My name is Annabel," the girl said. "I only wear those clothes and makeup and that wig to look cool. I just want people to like me. That's why I made those gargoyle videos, too. I wanted to be popular."

"We know that the gargoyles aren't real," said Jessie. "But your videos were fake, too?"

"They're fake," Annabel admitted. "Just

as fake as Raven was. I just acted like I saw gargoyles in the videos. I'd go to the library with a friend. He would hold the camera and I would pretend that the gargoyles appeared. And then tonight I *did* see a gargoyle."

"So you were pretending to be someone else," said Violet. "A made-up person..."

"Just like Holly Page," Henry said. "I bet we couldn't find Holly Page in those old yearbooks because *she's* a made-up person, too, just like Annabel was only acting like Raven."

"Annabel must be a pretty good actor," said Benny, "because your screams sounded really real."

"Oh, my screams *were* real tonight," said Annabel. "I really *did* see a gargoyle in the window just now. I wasn't filming this to put it online. The gargoyle I saw was real."

Jessie, Violet, and Benny didn't know whether to believe what Annabel was telling them—not after she hadn't been honest about everything else.

But Henry believed her. "We know that

gargoyles are just stone statues, but I think she's telling the truth, guys," he said, standing at the window. "She saw *something*. Look at this string hanging outside the glass. It looks like the string we saw at the library earlier tonight."

Sure enough, hanging outside the window was a string.

"It looks like the string is hanging from someplace above your room," Henry said.

"But the fourth floor is the top floor of Harper Hall," said Annabel. "The only thing above my room is the roof."

"Then we're headed to the roof," said Henry.

"That sounds like fun!" Benny shouted. "Let's go!"

"I'm sorry, guys," said Annabel. "My days of hunting gargoyles are done. I think I'll stay in my room. But if you want to get to the roof, take the stairs at the end of the hall. The door at the top opens out onto the roof—sometimes I go up there at night to watch the stars."

Benny had already started down the hall and up the stairs, so his sisters and brother had to run fast to catch up with him. They were all in such a hurry that no one heard the sound of footsteps running *down* the stairs, or the sound of the exit door opening and slamming shut.

The four Alden children went through the door at the top of the stairs and, sure enough, above them shined the moon and the constellations of the night sky.

"I see the Big Dipper!" Benny said.

"And look," said Jessie, "that constellation shaped like a hunter is called Orion."

"I wonder if Orion has ever gone gargoyle hunting like us," said Benny.

"I don't know," Henry said, "but I think we're pretty close to catching whoever is behind this mystery. Come on, the area right over there should be directly above Raven's, er, Annabel's room. Just be careful, since we're on the roof of a building."

The roof of Harper Hall was flat, but the children walked carefully to the edge.

"Here's the string," said Benny, holding one end of the string up in the air.

"So whoever is scaring people must be dangling the gargoyle from a string," Henry explained. "They must have used the same trick at the library, hanging the gargoyle that we saw from the window on the top floor."

"But those gargoyles are part of the library," said Jessie. "I don't see how somebody could pull a heavy stone statue off of a building and hang it from a little piece of string like a piñata at a birthday party."

Benny held the other end of the string in his hand. "It looks like this string is broken. The gargoyle must have fallen."

"Benny's right," Henry said, cautiously peeking over the edge of the roof. "I can see something in the bushes below."

"I see it, too," said Violet. "It's gray and has wings. It's a gargoyle!"

While Annabel had been frightened by the gargoyle that appeared at Harper Hall, the Alden children weren't scared at all. Back to the stairway door they hurried, and down the stairs to the ground floor they raced.

Once again, Benny led the way. Once he was through the door he ran and around the side of the dorm to the bushes they'd seen from the roof.

"It is a gargoyle!" Benny yelled. "And it's not heavy at all."

Henry, Jessie, and Violet turned the corner to see their little brother standing in the middle of a green, prickly bush. In Benny's hand was a gray, grinning gargoyle held high over his head.

"We can be sure that's not a real statue now," said Jessie.

"Yeah," said Henry. "Benny might be strong for a kid, but nobody could lift one of the real gargoyles over his head."

Violet looked puzzled. "That gargoyle looks just like the statues on top of the library, though. If it's not a real statue, what is it?"

Jessie took the gargoyle from Benny and helped her little brother out of the bushes. She tapped the grinning creature with her

finger. A dusting of white powder showered down from the bottom of the gargoyle. "This isn't made of stone," she said. "It's made out of papier-mâché."

"Papier-mâché!" said Violet. "I know where I've heard that word before. It was on a book at the library."

"Then we need to go back to the library so we can finally solve the mystery of the grinning gargoyles," Henry said.

"And we will," said Jessie, "just as soon as we get a good night's sleep. We have a very big day tomorrow."

The Alden children took the papier-mâché gargoyle with them as they headed back into Harper Hall. Leaving the papier-mâché gargoyle with Annabel—to show her it had been a sculpture and not a living, breathing creature outside her window—the Aldens headed back to suite 4A.

"I think Annabel had the right idea, wearing those pretty pajamas to bed," Violet yawned as the children reached the front door of their suite.

"That reminds me of something you said back in Annabel's room," said Henry, holding the door for his siblings. "You said Raven was a made-up person, and I realized that Holly Page was made-up, too. I've been thinking about that ever since, and I think there's someone whose name sounds a little bit like Holly and who spends the day looking through pages and pages."

"I think you're right, Henry," said Jessie. "And I think after we get some rest tonight, we know who to talk to."

CHAPTER 8

Checked Out

The next morning, Jessie woke her brothers and sister very early.

"I'm tired," said Benny. "We were up so late."

"We're going to be busy today," Jessie said. "There's the groundbreaking ceremony, and then the big game..."

"And we still have the mystery to solve, too," said Henry, stretching his arms and climbing out of bed. "Let's head right to the library."

"I'll leave a note for Grandfather," Violet said, pulling a purple pen and a pad of paper from her purple duffel bag. "We can meet him at the ceremony once we have finished our work."

On the way to the library, the Aldens stopped at the Bruin Beanery.

Behind the counter was a smiling girl with light-brown hair. On the girl's chest was a name badge that said Annabel.

"Hi, Raven!" said Benny. "I mean, Annabel. We're going to have a little breakfast before we go to the library."

"What would you like?" Annabel asked. "Breakfast is on the house."

"On the house?" Benny asked. "Don't you mean on the roof?"

Annabel laughed. "It means that whatever you kids want to eat for breakfast is free. It's my way of saying thank you for helping me last night when I was scared."

"Thank you," Violet said. "You're really nice, Annabel."

"Yeah," said Benny. "You're about the nicest suspect I've ever met!"

"Annabel's not a suspect," Henry said.

"Not anymore. But she can do one thing for us."

"What's that?" asked Annabel.

"You and your friend with the video camera can meet us after the groundbreaking ceremony for the Alden Library," said Henry. "You can film the final chapter of the grinning gargoyle mystery. Will you do that?"

"We sure will," Annabel said. "I didn't think I'd be making anymore gargoyle videos, but I suspect this is a good plan."

"Speaking of suspects," said Jessie, "I think we know which suspect we need to talk to. Let's eat our breakfast as we walk."

The Aldens had finished their breakfast by the time they reached the old library. The stone gargoyles grinned down at them from high above. The papier-mâché gargoyle he had found the night before grinned up at the statues from Benny's arms.

Benny held onto his gargoyle until the children reached the desk where Miss Hollenberg already sat. The old librarian looked up from the book she was reading and was surprised when the youngest Alden dropped the papier-mâché creature into her lap.

"Where did you get this gargoyle?" Miss Hollenberg asked, looking surprised and a little bit annoyed with the powdering of white dust that covered her red dress. "It's papier-mâché. Did you children make it?"

"No," said Henry. "But we think *you* did."

"Why would I do such a thing?" asked Miss Hollenberg.

"You're sad about the Alden Library replacing this old library," said Jessie, "and you thought you could foil the plan by scaring people with the legend of the grinning gargoyles."

Miss Hollenberg laughed. "Why that's the silliest thing I've ever heard," she said. "For one thing, the Alden Library isn't replacing anything. But that's a secret for today's ceremony, so that's all I will say about that. And for another thing, the legend of the grinning gargoyles is fiction..."

"What does 'fiction' mean?" Benny asked.

"It means 'made up,'" Henry said. "Just like Raven was made up. Or just like Holly Page, who wrote the newspaper article!"

"I haven't heard that name in years," Miss Hollenberg sighed, taking the old, yellowed newspaper from her desktop.

"You created the gargoyle legend, didn't you, Miss Hollenberg?" Violet asked. "You were Holly Page."

"I sure did," said Miss Hollenberg. She pointed to the author's name on the newspaper article. "See. Holly, like Hollenberg. And Page, like the pages in all these books Holly Page. That's me."

"But why would you make up a legend like that?" asked Jessie.

"Years ago, even before your grandfather was a student here at Goldwin University, I had a problem with students misbehaving in the library," Miss Hollenberg explained. "Like I told you when you arrived yesterday, gargoyles are supposed to protect the buildings which they decorate. I figured that a spooky legend about grinning gargoyles would make everyone behave. So I wrote this article in the Goldwin Gazette, using Holly Page as my pen name."

"What's a pen name?" Benny asked.

"It's a made-up name an author uses instead of their own," said Henry. "Sort of like how Annabel used the name Raven for her videos. Did your article work, Miss Hollenberg?"

"It did back then, and then it was forgotten for many, many years," said the old librarian. "But recently, the legend of the grinning gargoyles has been causing more trouble than it has solved, what with people talking about gargoyles scratching at windows and peeking in at scared students. It reminded me of the old article, which I found among my things. I don't know how anyone else knew about the legend, though—I highly doubt there are any other copies left."

"Then how would someone find out about the legend," Jessie wondered, "if they didn't have a copy of that old newspaper?"

"There are lots of other ways to find things

in the library," said Miss Hollenberg. "I'm sure someone found the article online…"

"You're probably right," said Henry, "because that's how we found it—on the computer last night. I think we have a pretty good idea who has been hanging gargoyles from windows, don't we?"

Violet and Benny nodded in agreement, while Jessie walked over to the carts of books parked by the elevator doors. She returned carrying the art book titled *Papier-mâché* that the children had seen the night before.

"Will you do us a favor, Miss Hollenberg?" Jessie asked.

"Certainly," said Miss Hollenberg.

"We can prove who the computer culprit is with the help of *your* computer," said Jessie. "Can you look up the person who last checked out this book? Whoever borrowed this book is behind the mystery of the grinning gargoyles."

Miss Hollenberg looked up the name and showed it to the Alden children. Then she looked at the time and said, "You might have a suspect to apprehend, but we all have a ceremony to attend."

"And there are also a couple things I think we want to discuss with Grandfather," said Jessie. "Things that will help Goldwin University be an even better place than it already is."

CHAPTER 9

Breaking Ground and Cracking the Case

Along with Miss Hollenberg, Henry, Jessie, Violet, and Benny Alden hurried out of the old library, looking up at the gargoyle statues grinning down from its top floor. A large crowd was already gathered on the empty lot next to the library.

"I see Coach Woods and the football team," said Violet.

"There is Grandfather," Benny said. "He's holding some kind of shiny shovel."

James Alden, proud graduate of Goldwin

University, did hold a shiny silver shovel in his hands. He stood at the front of the crowd, in front of a microphone, wearing his white suit and his tie that was the color of the red, autumn leaves. Grandfather Alden nodded to his grandchildren, and began his speech.

"Friends and family, students and teachers, I would like to welcome you all to this ground-breaking ceremony," he began.

"When I attended Goldwin University many, many years ago, I often came to this library building to study. I studied hard, and I have done well for myself. So it is only right that I give back to this special place that helped me learn and grow."

Grandfather Alden stuck the shovel into the ground and dug up a chunk of dirt. "With this ceremonial shovel full of earth, I begin the building of a new library, where students will be able to learn and grow for many years to come. But I will say, that this old library with its grinning gargoyle statues is very dear to me. I was reminded of this not only by this visit, but also by my dear friend Miss Hollenberg and by my four special grandchildren. I do not want the old library to be torn down and forgotten. So I propose that a walkway be built between the new library and the old one, to remind us of the past even as we look to the future. With both library buildings, Goldwin University will be able to house twice the books and twice the computers for its students to use."

The crowd broke into applause. The building of the Alden Library had begun, and the old library would still be used and appreciated. The children were proud of their grandfather.

But Grandfather Alden's speech was not finished yet. "I have another announcement," he said into the microphone. "I also hadn't realized that Goldwin Coliseum has fallen into disrepair..."

"What does that mean?" Benny asked Henry.

"It means that the football stadium is getting old," Henry explained.

"I would not only like to help with the building of a new library for the university to enjoy, but a new football stadium, as well," Grandfather Alden continued. "Using the money that would have been used to tear down the old library and build something else in its place, a new home for the Goldwin Bears football team can be built. It will still have a large video screen, but will also have comfortable seats, a well-groomed field, and facilities that are modern and well-kept..."

"And what does that mean?" asked Benny.

"It means that the new stadium's steps won't be crumbly and that the plumbing won't leak," said Jessie.

"This new sports arena shall be called Woods Stadium," Grandfather Alden said, "in honor of my good friend, our legendary Coach Woods."

The crowd applauded again, cheering for the coach, who looked very happy and quite shocked at the kind news.

"And with that," said Grandfather, "let's all head over and cheer for our Goldwin

Bears football team as they try to win the big game!"

The crowd cheered its loudest, and then the people started to walk across campus to Goldwin Coliseum.

Before the first of their remaining suspects could leave, the Alden children stopped Coach Woods.

"Good luck in the big game," said Henry.

"And good job on not being one of our suspects anymore," said Benny.

Coach Woods looked puzzled.

"I think what Benny meant is congratulations on the new stadium," said Jessie.

"It's going to be named after you!" said Violet.

"Did you come up with any big plays for the big game?" asked Benny.

"You will just have to come see for yourself," said Coach Woods. He thanked the children for their kind words, and then jogged to catch up with the players on his team.

The Alden children had now crossed three suspects off of their list—neither Coach

Woods, Miss Hollenberg, or Annabel was behind the gargoyle mystery. But their final suspect hadn't attended the ceremony.

"Come on, guys," Henry said, "we have a stop to make before we go to the game."

The children then paid a visit to Goldwin Gyros. The restaurant was empty, but the sound of pots and pans clattering came from the kitchen in back.

"Hello, children." Izzy said from the kitchen, sweat pouring from his bald head as he stood over the stove. "How are you this morning? I hope you haven't seen any gargoyles, other than the ones on the library."

"That's the thing," said Henry, "we *did* see a gargoyle last night. We saw it in the bushes outside of Harper Hall."

"That's ridiculous," said Izzy. "Gargoyles are just statues made of stone."

"Unless they're made out of papier-mâché," said a voice from behind the Alden children.

It was Annabel! Dressed in her black "Raven" clothes, but without her makeup or black wig. The Aldens' friend was followed by her cameraman.

"Hello, my online friends and fans," she said, "this is Annabel coming to you live from Goldwin University's favorite eatery—besides the Bruin Beanery, of course—Goldwin Gyros. Today I have the breaking story of the Grinning Gargoyles mystery, and the four young detectives who solved it."

With that, Annabel dropped the papier-mâché gargoyle the children had found the night before onto one of Izzy's kitchen counters.

"I guess I left something behind, didn't I?" said Izzy. "I am usually very good picking up after myself."

Jessie, who was also good about picking up after herself and her siblings, nodded. "We know that you are the person who has been scaring everyone with the legend of the grinning gargoyles," she said.

"You seemed so nice," said Benny, "and you made the best Gargoyle Gyro. So why were you scaring people?"

"I did it *because* of the Gargoyle Gyro," Izzy said. "You see, I was worried that after my father retired, nobody would come to this restaurant. Because I'm an artist, I have always loved the gargoyles on the old library. One day I did an online search to learn more about those grinning gargoyles, and I found an old newspaper article about the spooky gargoyle legend. It gave me the idea for the Gargoyle Gyro, as well as a way to get everyone talking about gargoyles."

"That's when you checked out the book on papier-mâché," said Jessie, "a month ago."

"I might be an artist," Izzy said, "but I'd never made anything out of papier-mâché before. The book taught me how to create the fake gargoyle I hung from the top floor of the library."

"Your gargoyle looks really good," said Violet, patting the papier-mâché creature. "It looks just like the real statues. But it also scared people, and that wasn't very nice."

"I'm sorry," Izzy said. "I didn't mean to scare anyone."

"There's someone you should really apologize to," said Jessie, motioning to Annabel. "It was Annabel's window that you hung the gargoyle in front of last night, and it really scared her."

"Oh, dear," said Izzy. "I was trying to put the gargoyle in front of *your* window, Alden children. I already knew you weren't scared of the gargoyles, so I figured it wouldn't hurt."

"We were staying in 4A, right next door to Annabel's room in 4B," Henry said.

"I am so sorry, Annabel," said Izzy. "How can I make it up to you?"

"It's okay, Izzy," Annabel smiled. "There *is* one thing you can do, though—an interview for this latest online video. It'll be a hit with my fans *and* it'll bring more business to Goldwin Gyros! Are you camera shy?"

CHAPTER 10

The Big Screen at the Big Game

The Goldwin Bears got off to a good start, even though Number 44 was sitting on the bench and hadn't played.

The clock was running down before halftime as Benny Alden returned to the red metal bleacher he'd been sitting on. In his arms he carried a stack of stadium snacks to share with his siblings.

Henry thanked Benny for the hot dog with extra mustard.

Jessie smiled and took a bite of her salty soft pretzel.

Violet wiped her mouth after taking a sip of her hot chocolate.

And Benny took turns putting popcorn and peanuts into his mouth.

Just then, the crowd began to cheer. From the bench where the Goldwin Bears were sitting a familiar player stood up and started to trot onto the field.

"Go, Number 44!" Benny cheered.

The Goldwin Bears lined up to run their next play. The play began, with players of both teams scurrying across the grass of Goldwin Coliseum.

The Bears' quarterback got the ball and took a step backward, staring down the field. He looked right. Then he looked left. Would he find someone who could catch the football?

And then, just like the play Coach Woods had drawn on the chalkboard at the library, and just like the play Benny had run on the field the day before, Number 44 streaked down the field. His ankle seemed to be better, allowing him to run fast across the grass.

The quarterback reared back and threw the football.

Up, up, up into the air went the ball.

Then down, down, down it came.

Number 44 leaped into the air, too, stretching out his arms and diving for the football.

It looked like the quarterback might have thrown the ball too far. Or maybe Number 44 wasn't able to run quite as fast as he needed to.

The ball looked like it would fall just out of the reach of the star player's outstretched fingertips.

And then those fingertips stretched just a little bit further, and Number 44 caught the ball, rolling into the end zone, just as the clock on the big screen reached zero.

Touchdown!

The crowd cheered.

Benny Alden looked up at the screen, hoping to see a replay. But instead, the screen began to show a very interesting halftime show.

There on the screen, in front of thousands of happy fans, were Henry, Jessie, Violet, and Benny Alden.

"That's me!" Benny said. "Up there on the screen!"

And next to the four Alden children stood two familiar faces.

"Hello, Goldwin University. My name is Annabel," a smiling girl with light-brown hair said to the camera. "But you might know me better as Raven, the girl in all of the gargoyle videos you've watched on the Internet."

The crowd cheered—they had seen Raven's videos.

"Well, the mystery of the grinning gargoyles has been solved, just like I promised it would be on my last video," Annabel said.

The crowd gasped—they wanted to know how the mystery ended.

"Although I wanted to be the one to solve the mystery," said Annabel, "my four friends here proved that they are better detectives than I could ever be. I'd like to introduce you to Henry, Jessie, Violet, and Benny Alden."

The crowd roared their approval—for the Alden children waving to them from the big screen, as well as the Alden children sitting with them in Goldwin Coliseum.

Annabel smiled on the big screen and said, "I now give you, the man behind the mystery, the man behind the grinning gargoyles, and the man behind the Gargoyle Gyro—Izzy, the owner of Goldwin Gyros!"

Izzy was on the video, too. He twirled his mustache and wiped a hand over his bald head, then began to speak. "I would like to apologize to everyone who might have been scared of the gargoyles. They were not real. I only wanted to let everyone know about the good food I would like to share with you. And now I hope you not only appreciate the great gargoyle statues we are lucky to have here at Goldwin University, but that you enjoy the free Gargoyle Gyros I will be serving at my restaurant after the game."

The crowd screamed at the top of their lungs and stomped their feet and clapped their hands—for the end of the mystery and

for the promise of free food.

The video ended with Izzy, Annabel, and the Alden children waving to the camera.

And the big game ended with Goldwin University winning 28-0.

As the Alden family walked to Goldwin Gyros after the game, Benny smiled and said, "Grandfather, I can't wait until next year when we can come watch the big game at the brand new Woods Stadium. Although the only gargoyle I want grinning at me is a Gargoyle Gyro!"

THE BOXCAR CHILDREN

For more about the Boxcar Children,
visit them online at

TheBoxcarChildren.com

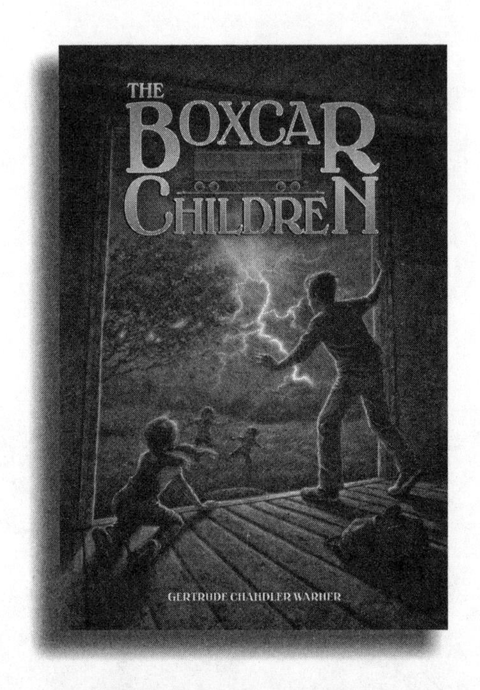

#1 THE BOXCAR CHILDREN
THE BOXCAR CHILDREN® MYSTERIES
HC 978-0-8075-0851-0
$15.99/$17.99 Canada
PB 978-0-8075-0852-7
$5.99/$6.99 Canada
"One warm night four children stood in front of a bakery. No one knew them. No one knew where they had come from." So begins Gertrude Chandler Warner's beloved story about four orphans who run away and find shelter in an abandoned boxcar. There they manage to live all on their own, and at last, find love and security from an unexpected source.

#2 SURPRISE ISLAND
THE BOXCAR CHILDREN® MYSTERIES

HC 978-0-8075-7673-1
$15.99/$17.99 Canada
PB 978-0-8075-7674-8
$5.99/$6.99 Canada

The Boxcar Children have a home with their grandfather now—but their adventures are just beginning! Their first adventure is to spend the summer camping on their own private island. The island is full of surprises, including a kind stranger with a secret.

THE BOXCAR CHILDREN BEGINNING

by Patricia MacLachlan

Before they were the Boxcar Children,Henry, Jessie, Violet, and Benny Alden lived with their parents on Fair Meadow Farm.

978-0-8075-6617-6
US $5.99 paperback

Although times are hard, they're happy—"the best family of all," Mama likes to say. And when a traveling family needs shelter from a winter storm, the Aldens help, and make new friends. But the spring and summer bring events that will change all their lives forever.

Newbery Award-winning author Patricia MacLachlan tells a wonderfully moving story of the Alden children's origins.

* * *

"Fans will enjoy this picture of life 'before.'"—*Publishers Weekly*

"An approachable lead-in that serves to fill in the background both for confirmed fans and readers new to the series." —*Kirkus Reviews*

Gertrude Chandler Warner discovered when she was teaching that many readers who like an exciting story could find no books that were both easy and fun to read. She decided to try to meet this need, and her first book, *The Boxcar Children*, quickly proved she had succeeded.

Miss Warner drew on her own experiences to write the mystery. As a child she spent hours watching trains go by on the tracks opposite her family home. She often dreamed about what it would be like to set up housekeeping in a caboose or freight car—the situation the Alden children find themselves in.

While the mystery element is central to each of Miss Warner's books, she never thought of them as strictly juvenile mysteries. She liked to stress the Aldens' independence and resourcefulness and their solid New England devotion to using up and making do. The Aldens go about most of their adventures with as little adult supervision as possible—something else that delights young readers.

Miss Warner lived in Putnam, Connecticut, until her death in 1979. During her lifetime, she received hundreds of letters from girls and boys telling her how much they liked her books.